For Margy and Dan Becker and all parents and adults like them
who fuel the passion of play and believe in the dreams of children

K. M. B.

For Tanei

J. H.

Text copyright © 2013 by KaBOOM!
Illustrations copyright © 2013 by Jed Henry

First edition 2013

Library of Congress Catalog Card Number 2012947706
ISBN 978-0-7636-5531-0

13 14 15 16 17 18 TLF 10 9 8 7 6 5 4 3 2 1

Printed in Dongguan, Guangdong, China

This book was typeset in Cafeteria.
The illustrations were created digitally.

Candlewick Press
99 Dover Street
Somerville, Massachusetts 02144

visit us at www.candlewick.com

My Dream Playground

A  Book

Kate M. Becker

illustrated by Jed Henry

CANDLEWICK PRESS

I dream about having a playground—a real playground, a fun playground—in our neighborhood. But all we have is an empty lot down the street from my apartment.

I know that someday my dream is going to come true.

Every day on my way home from school, I walk past the empty lot and then I run up the steps and into our apartment. I grab my pencils, crayons, and sketchpad, and then I head back down to the stoop and start to draw. What I draw is my dream playground.

I draw slides

and swings

and monkey bars

and trampolines.

I draw my friends and my brothers sliding down the twisty slide,

jumping on the trampoline, and flying as high as the buildings.

I show my drawings to my mom, and she hangs them on our fridge.
"Never stop dreaming," she tells me.

Then after dinner, my brothers and I add to my drawings. We use purple for the slide, yellow for the swings, and red for the trampoline. Right now our drawings are just dreams, but I know that someday they will come true.

Then one day, everything changes. My brothers and I are sitting on our stoop when a man comes by and stops to look around the empty lot across the street.

"It's him!" I say.

"Who?" my brothers ask.

"The man who is going to build our playground!"

He takes out a tape measure and starts measuring and making notes
on a clipboard.

I run up the steps two at a time and into our apartment. I grab my
drawings from the fridge and rush back down the stairs.

"Excuse me, sir," I say to the man. "You're here to build the playground, aren't you?" He looks surprised at first, and then he smiles.

"Yes. Yes, I am," he tells me. "How did you know?"

"I just knew," I say. "I just knew you would come."

"Well, you're right. My name is Darell, and some hardworking volunteers are going to turn this vacant lot into a playground."

"Can I show you some of my designs?" I ask nervously.

"Designs?"

"For the playground. I always dreamed a playground would get built here."

I show him my drawings, and he looks them over carefully. Then he says, "You are a talented architect! This is an impressive playground design! How would you like to be a project manager? We could use your help."

"Really?" I say. "I can be a hardworking volunteer, too!" Then Darell and I shake hands.

The next day, I run home as soon as school is out. Darell is already at the lot, and he hands me my very own clipboard. "Here you go, Project Manager!" he says.

Darell asks my opinion on everything!

"How many slides do we need?" he asks.

"Two," I say.

"Monkey bars or swings?"

"Both."

Then I make more designs on my clipboard and show them to Darell.

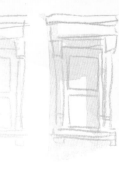

Once we've decided on everything, Darell asks me to make one more drawing—the final design for our new playground. Except this one is going to be real and not a dream.

After days and weeks and months of being a project manager and planning for my dream playground, the time to build it is finally here. Hundreds of people come to help, including just about everybody I know—plus lots and lots of people I don't know.

Mr. Sid from the market brings the sandwiches. Ms. Gonzalez from the hardware store brings the tent. Gregory from upstairs is playing music. It's a big party. And everyone is working.

We cut wood, dig holes,

hammer, and paint.

When it starts raining, we keep working, regardless of the mud. And that's even more fun.

It takes a whole week to build everything, but at last we're done! A huge crowd gathers to cheer for us. There is even a TV camera, and a reporter interviews me for the news! My name is in the newspaper, and so is a picture of our playground!

But the best part of all is playing on the playground that I helped build.
My dream playground came true, just like I knew it would!

Author's Note

Every child should have a great place to play within walking distance. That is what KaBOOM! believes and why it exists. KaBOOM! is a national nonprofit that was founded by Darell Hammond.

The hero in this story is inspired by a real girl named Ashley. In 1995, Darell Hammond moved to Washington, D.C., to plan a service project for volunteers who would be attending a conference. He decided to build a playground and selected Livingston Manor in Washington, D.C., for this project. Darell planned the project so that the volunteers from outside the community would work side by side with community members.

Just like the narrator of this story, Ashley ran to Darell on his first day there and showed him her designs for her dream playground. After Darell made her a project manager, Ashley collected pennies for the playground, coaxed her family and neighbors to get involved, and worked tirelessly to make the project happen.

KaBOOM! believes in the dreams and imaginations of children. When you put the power and resources of communities and local leaders behind a child's dream, there is an explosion of hope and possibility. That is what we call KaBOOM!

For more information, go to kaboom.org.

To plan your own dream playground, go to ourdreamplayground.org.

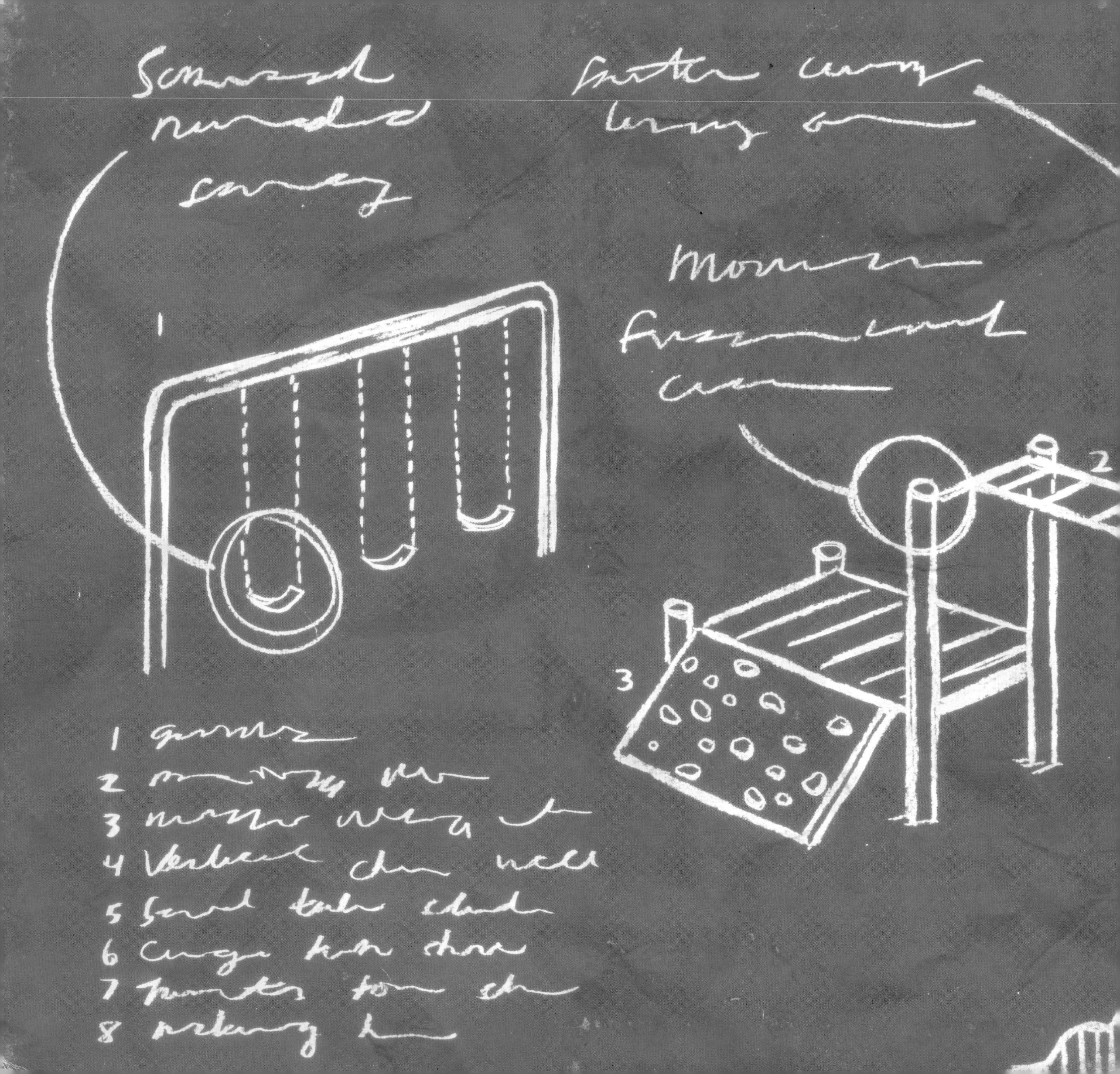
1
2
3